The Strangest Robbery

Nicolette Powers

The Strangest Robbery

East Texas 1899

Nicolette & David Powers

CROSSBOOKS

CrossBooks™
A Division of LifeWay
1663 Liberty Drive
Bloomington, IN 47403
www.crossbooks.com
Phone: 1-866-879-0502

© 2013 Nicolette & David Powers. All rights reserved.

No part of this book may be reproduced, stored in a retrieval system, or transmitted by any means without the written permission of the author.

First published by CrossBooks 3/11/2013

ISBN: 978-1-4627-2525-0 (sc)
ISBN: 978-1-4627-2526-7 (e)

Printed in the United States of America

This book is printed on acid-free paper.

Any people depicted in stock imagery provided by Thinkstock are models, and such images are being used for illustrative purposes only.

Certain stock imagery © Thinkstock.

Because of the dynamic nature of the Internet, any web addresses or links contained in this book may have changed since publication and may no longer be valid. The views expressed in this work are solely those of the author and do not necessarily reflect the views of the publisher, and the publisher hereby disclaims any responsibility for them.

For both of my fathers, one spiritual and the other physical.
—Nicolette

For my parents and Jesus.
—David

CONTENTS

Chapter 1   Meet the Richards 1

Chapter 2   Life with the Richards. 9

Chapter 3   The Rig 21

Chapter 4   Salvation 27

Chapter 5   A Rope is Found 33

Chapter 6   Tom Takes a Tumble. 37

Chapter 7   Mr. Richards Camps Out 41

Chapter 8   A Swing is Hung. 45

Chapter 9   The Big Holdup 51

Chapter 10 The Mystery is Solved 59

Chapter 1

Meet the Richards

Sweat burned in the eyes of fourteen year old Charles Wilson. "Get up Chess," Charles said to his horse, Chess. The chestnut horse just snorted. "I hear there's an oil rig and a town up there. Maybe I can get some food for you and me." After a minute or two Charles spotted at a stream. "Whoa, Chess, we can get some water right here." Charles tramped over to the stream. The stream was muddy and hot, but Charles washed his hands and face. Then he filled his bottle anyway. Charles looked up and said, "Chess, I can see the derrick. We should be there by this afternoon."

The hours went by slowly. Finally they were at the edge of town, when someone said, "You are ugly and filthy!" Charles almost fell out of the saddle. He looked over and saw a girl with her hands on her hips. "Why are you so filthy?" the girl asked, with her nose turned up. "Why do you want to know?" Charles said glaring at her, "Well, if you are going to answer my questions with questions, you can get out of my way so I can get some flour." The girl said shortly. Charles rode forward a little ways, when he heard a soft voice call to him, "Where are you going?" Charles glanced around, his eyes fixed on a small lady standing in the doorway of a middle sized brown house. "Do you want some supper?" she asked "Y-y-yes ma'am." he stuttered. "Then take that horse around back and put it in the barn. You can brush it and feed it too." The lady told him. "Yes, ma'am." Charles said.

The lady disappeared into the house. Charles led Chess around back to the barn. "Why is this lady being so nice to us, boy?" Charles asked his horse, as he brushed at the horse's tangled mane. Chess snorted and continued to eat his oats. Charles put the brush away and headed for the house.

As he walked to the house, the lady stuck her head out. She said, "Come here, boy. You need a bath," she said. Charles ran toward her. When he reached the house, he walked through the open door. A tub of steaming water stood waiting. The lady was nowhere to be seen. Suddenly the door swung open, "Why do you just stand there, boy?" the lady said "I –I- I," embarrassed, Charles stammered. "Never mind boy, just bathe and put on these clothes," she said. "Yes, ma'am." Charles said, the lady left, closing the door behind her.

Charles scrubbed himself from head to toe. He didn't want to come back and try again. After he finished, he dressed and knocked on the door. "Come in," the lady called. So Charles went into the cozy kitchen. "Now, first things first. My name is Mrs. Richards, what is yours?" she asked. "My name is Charles, Charles Wilson." Charles replied. "Well Charles, why don't you set the table while I finish dinner?" Mrs. Richards asked. "Yes, ma'am," Charles replied. Seeing an open cabinet door, Charles looked inside and set the table with plates and glasses.

Charles was setting the last plate on the table when he heard the back door bang shut. I feel like hiding! Charles thought No telling who else lives in this family. Just then a girl stepped in. "Mother, they raised the price of flour again!" the girl said, a bonnet hiding her face. She pulled the bonnet off and started to move forward, but spotting Charles, she froze. "What is he doing here?" she asked. "You mean Charles Wilson? Why he's our special guest for tonight." Mrs. Richards replied pleasantly. You could here a pin drop as Charles and the girl eyed each other.

Mrs. Richards finally broke the silence with two commands. "Alice, you finish the table. Charles you go get the flour." Alice shuffled around one side of the table as Charles bolted around the other. Charles was outside and to the standing wheelbarrow in two seconds flat. He hoisted the flour sack onto his shoulder. He had only taken one step back when he heard the front door shut. He paused, wondering whom it could be. "Henry, your home!" Mrs. Richards called.

Charles started towards the house again. From inside the house he heard, "Alice, you look like a cow staring at a new gate." "Mom invited some bum off the streets to supper!" the girl wailed. Charles heard Mrs. Richards scolding Alice, as he slowly made his way to the house. "Alice, you shouldn't talk about Charles that way! For all you know he's a fine gentleman down on his luck. And he's no bum for sure, bums don't run to fulfill orders." Charles opened the door. "Besides, you know what the Bible says about that; Hebrews 13:2 'Be not forgetful to entertain strangers: for thereby some have entertained angels unawares.'" Douse it really? Charles thought, well, I'm definitely not an angel!

When he stepped inside, a tall man turned from where he stood leaning on the table. "Well here's Charles now. Hello, young man," the tall man boomed. Mrs. Richards called to Charles, "Bring the flour over here Charley, you don't mind if I call you Charley do you?" "No ma'am," Charles lowered the flour sack to where she motioned. He guessed the large tin with the scoop was where the flour was kept.

"Alice, come and help me serve the food." Mrs. Richards said. As Mrs. Richards passed Charles, she told him to go have a seat. Alice passed him as well. "Bum," she said under her breath. Charles walked to the table, and glanced from place to place, unsure where to sit.

3

Mr. Richards motioned to the three open chairs "Have a seat wherever you like son, only don't sit there, (pointing to the chair beside him) or there, (pointing to the chair across from him)." Mr. Richards slapped his leg roaring with laughter. Charles laughed too, taking the chair across from Mrs. Richards.

Soon Alice and Mrs. Richards appeared with steaming dishes. After setting the food on the table, they had a seat. Mr. Richards said grace and the food were served. How good the food smelled to Charles, how hungry he was! There was a moment of silence as everybody ate his or her food.

Finally Mr. Richards broke the silence with the question the whole Richards family was dying to know, "Where is your ma and pa?" "I don't got any now." Charles replied. After a silent spell, the Richards family all burst forth with a litany of questions. When, where, and how did you lose your parents? Charles answered, "I'm not sure I can answer all those questions but I can tell you what I know. Mom passed away when I was too young to remember. But I know she died of the fever. Dad died later in the hospital of the fever when I was ten. I wasn't there, a nurse came and told me. Then she ordered me to get my stuff and tie them to Chess, 'cause I was going to the orphanage. So I got my stuff, saddled Chess and off we rode.

When we got there, I was given to a grouch of a housemother, as they called them. There were nine of us. I didn't last one day in that place. When night came I ran away. We were going to bed when she came in and started yelling at us. Then, she started throwing things and hitting us with a broom. She punched a kid right in the face he fell on the ground crying three more followed by broom or fist. When I got hit I got angry. I yelled back, "I'm not going to stay if things are going to be thrown at me." I turned and jumped out the window smashing it in the process. Like lighting I ran to the shed and put a bit in Chess's mouth and jumped on him.

We bolted out of the shed, around the house and toward the gate. Suddenly a man from nowhere jumped out and shut the gate. I went to pull the reins, but wasn't fast enough. Good thing too, because Chess jumped right over the gate. We galloped down the street and off into the night. I never looked back. I was only ten when that happened."

Mr. Richards waved his fork in the air, "That's some story boy," he said. Mrs. Richards said nothing. Charles glanced at Alice out of the corner of his eye. She was scowling. The look on her face said, "I don't believe one word he just said." It was plain to see that if Alice had anything to do with it, he was out of there. Alice voiced her opinion, "I thought you were orphanage trash". "Alice!" Mrs. Richards gasped. No one spoke for the rest of the meal.

When supper was over, Mrs. Richards told Alice to clear the table, to Charles she said, "I'm going to show you where you are to sleep." Charles followed Mrs. Richards to the bedroom, while Alice cleared off the table. "The room down the hall is mine, and the room just before is Alice's. Charles stood there looking. "Well go in and look around." Mrs. Richards said. "Yes ma'am," he said as he walked in. He saw a small bed, an old dresser, and a closet. He hurried out. "Well you weren't in there long. How clean was the window?" Mrs. Richards asked. "There's a window in there?" Charles asked. "Yes there's a window in there." she replied.

"You know, how would you feel if we took you shopping tomorrow?" she asked. "Well, I don't have any money for stuff like that." Charles said. "That's alright, I think we can afford to cover you this time." Mrs. Richards said. "Oh no, I can't let you do that ma'am." Charles exclaimed. *I will not mooch!* Charles thought. "Fine, have it your way. You will go shopping in the morning, and work for Mr. Richards after lunch." she said. "Yes ma'am" he replied. "Okay, let's go back and see what the rest of the family is doing." she said. They walked back down the hall into the living room. Mr. Richards looked up from his paper and said, "I'm going to enroll him in school as soon as possible, if he doesn't mind." "I'm O.K. with that." Charles stammered. "Good, how about Mother and you go shopping before lunch and afterward

5

you can come and work at the oil rig?" Mr. Richards declared. "Yes, sir." Charles answered. "Now to the business at hand, soon as Alice gets done with those dishes, we'll read the Bible." Mr. Richards said loudly. "I'm hurrying Daddy," Alice shouted back.

"Son, someone has been stealing my oil and I don't know who it is. So keep an eye out while you're helping me." "Yes, sir." Charles said stiffly. Alice came into the room with Bibles in her hands. Mr. Richards leaned over and said quietly "How about you have a seat and when Alice hands you a Bible say she has tow hair." "Yes, sir." Charles whispered back.

Charles walked over and took a seat. "Pass out the Bibles please, Alice." Mrs. Richards said to her daughter. Alice handed her mother and father their Bibles and picked up her own. "Shall I get the boy one?" Alice asked. "Of course you should get Charley one." Mrs. Richards replied somewhat sharply. Alice turned on her heel and left the room to get a new Bible. She took her own sweet time about it too. When she finally returned she had a new leather Bible in her hand. "Here," she said holding out the new Bible. "Thank you, little Miss towhead." Charles said with a sly grin. "How dare you call me that?" Alice shrieked. She drew back and, wham! hit Charles in the head with the bible! Charles didn't know what hit him. He fell backwards in the chair, surprised. When he sat up, he saw his reflection in the big looking glass on the wall. His forehead said, 'Holy Bible KJV'. "Alice go to your room this instant." Mrs. Richards said sternly. Alice set the Bible down and with the air of a queen, she slid out of the room.

As soon as she was gone, Mr. Richards started laughing. Mrs. Richards shook her head and turned to Charles. "Are you O.K. Charley?" she asked. "Oh, yes ma'am," he said, still a bit stunned. "I guess I pressed her a bit much?" Charles asked. "No, only the next time you try her get ready to duck." Mr. Richards said still laughing. They read the Bible peacefully after that, and went off to their rooms. Perhaps I ought to apologize to Alice, Charles thought. Naw, I'd

THE STRANGEST ROBBERY

better give her till morning, she's liable to knock me out. He yawned and glanced about his room. Hey, there is a window, cool. These folks sure are nice to put me up. I guess I won't knock out this window unless of course Alice comes after me. Yikes! Thinking about that could give a fellow nightmares. Charles changed, hopped into bed and fell right to sleep.

Chapter 2

Life with the Richards

THE BRIGHT SUNLIGHT AND A far away whinny woke Charles from his slumber the next morning. "Oh, Chess, here boy." Charles mumbled. "I need to get out of this cave." Crawling to the edge of the... WHOOMP!! He landed on his face on the floor. Where am I? He wondered, while worming his way out of the sheets. Charles sat up, rubbed his eyes and looked about himself. Oh yeah, duh! I'm at the Richard's, Charles thought. He slipped out of his nightshirt given to him by Mrs. Richards, and into his own clothes. He pulled a comb through his hair, made his bed and ran into the kitchen almost petrified at the thought of missing breakfast, because he knew it would be a good one.

Mrs. Richards was just tying on her apron. "Well, well you're up early. Alice and Mr. Richards won't be up for another fifteen to thirty minutes." She said. "What can I do to help?" Charles asked. "Well

Charley, do you suppose you could get me some eggs from the coop?" she asked. "Yes ma'am I can do that!" he replied as he shot out the back door. He ran around the yard wondering where the coop was.

Thinking to himself it's probably behind the barn, he rounded the corner of the barn at top speed, Bam! Chickens flapped and cackled and a dog ran away barking, while Charles picked himself up off the ground. Looking around to see if anyone was watching, he thought, well, it was behind the barn after all. He opened the coop door and grabbed a few eggs, and ran back to the house.

When he got inside Mrs. Richards gave him a curious look. "Give me those eggs and go wash up." She said. He handed off the eggs and went outside to the well. *I wonder if Mrs. Richards could tell I fell down, probably so.* Thinking to himself as he lowered the bucket into the well, *I guess Mr. Richards and Alice will be getting up soon, so I'd better just take some water to the house. He slowly pulled the bucket up from the well. Boy I don't know how I will endure a shopping trip, especially if Alice comes;* he contemplated this while washing his hands and face. Dumping the rest out he lowered the bucket for the last time before going in again. *I'll take this back to Mrs. Richards, I'm sure she'll need it.* Charles thought. He drew the bucket up and tried not to splash too much out as he made his way to the house.

It was not long after that Mr. Richards and Alice got up. After eating a hardy breakfast Mrs. Richards, Charles and Alice headed for the barn. As they loaded up in the wagon Mr. Richards joked, "Charles, the gals will get you fixed up. School starts in fall though, so be patient. It ain't manly to try on lots of clothes. So, if anyone walks toward you, just hide behind the racks." Everyone laughed and they started off for town at a trot.

Mrs. Richards sat in the front of the wagon, while Alice and Charles occupied the back. Alice smoothed down her skirt, straightened her hat, and rearranged her curls. "I'm ready to accept your apology," she said. *I never said anything about apologizing to her; I'd better pretend*

I didn't hear her. Charles thought. He turned and looked out the side of the wagon.

Alice gave him a minute, and then cleared her throat. No response. Alice tapped her foot and cleared her throat again, still no response. Alice glanced at Charles out of the corner of her eyes and said, "You'd better answer me." Charles turned and said, in his most courteous voice, "Mind if I ask who you're talking to?" "No, I do not." she replied visibly irritated. "Then Missy, who ya talking to?" "You, bum!" Alice snapped back. She spoke so loudly Mrs. Richards heard. "Alice Joy Richards!" Mrs. Richards said angrily.

Reaching forward she grabbed the horsewhip and turned it upside down. She swung it backwards, only at the wrong side of the wagon, and smacked Charley atop the head. Alice snickered. "Do not sass me!" Mrs. Richards barked, smacking Charley in the head again. "But," Charley yelped. "I said not to sass me," Mrs. Richards said while taking another swing. This time Charles didn't wait to be hit again, he jumped into the front seat, and let the whip crash into the back seat. "Alice, you moved!" Mrs. Richards said "No." Alice answered honestly. Mrs. Richards started to turn but stopped upon seeing Charles. "What are you doing up here Charley?" she asked quizzically. "You were smacking me instead of Alice." Charles explained while rubbing his head. "Oh goodness, I'm sorry." Mrs. Richards said with her eyes growing wide. Then she smiled, stifled a laugh and said to Charles "Drive the horses, Alice and I have an appointment." All Charles heard was a smack. They rode along in silence until Charles leaned back and said; "I'm sorry," Alice smiled. "That you're a mean little towhead." He added, Alice seethed.

The store came into view. Mrs. Richards said, "Turn in there." she pointed at the store. Charles turned in; his eyes took in all the surroundings. The store was a big log cabin with hitching rails in front, and people standing in little groups and talking. He jumped to the ground and tied the horses up.

Alice and Mrs. Richards climbed down and headed for the store. Charles hurried to catch up. Mrs. Richards smiled and then turned to examine some gloves for sale out front.

Alice motioned for him to follow her. She stepped up behind some racks of clothes, Charles followed. "I'll just forgive you and we can both move on." Alice said. "OK." Charles replied grinning. "Good, I'll show you around and get you acquainted. Mother always pokes around just about forever at the sales." She headed for the door and paused, "Mother! I'm taking Charles inside." She grabbed Charles' sleeve and pulled him through the revolving door before Mrs. Richards had a chance to respond.

"Oh, what fun! I just love shopping don't you?" Alice chattered. "Hum-mm," Charles started, but Alice went on, "You'll be looking sharp before this day is out." Alice continued talking nonstop as she skipped to the back of the store where the men's section was. "Mm-mm, what size are you?"

C. "I don't know."

A. "Well look."

C. "At what?"

A. "The tag of course."

C. "OK."

Charles grabbed a pair of pants off the shelf and looked at the tag. Alice rolled her eyes.

"You are trying my patience Charles."

She grabbed him by the collar and pulled him down to read where his shirt tags should have been.

A. "There's no tag."

C. "Now what do we do?"

A. "You get to try on everything."

C. "Oh, really?"

A. "Yes really."

C. "Where do we start?"

A. "30-34."

She handed him a pair of pants and a shirt,"Go try them on." she instructed.

"Where?"

"In the boys dressing room."

"Oh." he said dryly starting for the dressing room and thinking, I hope nobody sees me.

He slipped into the clothes and peeked his head out. "Come on over!" Alice shouted. "Shh!" Charles whispered. "What?" Alice hollered, "I said..." Charles stomped over to her "Shut up!" Alice grinned, "That looks nice but I think you need a dark red shirt not a pink one."

C. "You picked it out."

A. "So?"

C. "Where's your Ma?"

"Oh, she'll be in here any minute now, but she'll laugh if you don't go and change out of the pink." Alice grinned. Charles stomped away with a dust brown colored shirt. When he came back Mrs. Richards was there. "My, my! Doesn't Alice have you looking nice." She commented. Alice smiled and said, "Yep, that outfit is a keeper. Now go try these on." Charles groaned realizing that Alice would have him try on clothes all day. "You know what size I wear so just pick out some clothes and let's be on our way." He suggested, "Just go try these on." Alice said. Seeing he was getting nowhere, he turned and went back to the dressing room to try some more on.

When he returned Mrs. Richards was no where to be found and Alice had a pile of clothes so big he was sure it would be impossible to try them all on in a single day. He considered asking if he had to try them all on, but changed his mind.

C. "I'm not trying all these on."

A. "Yes you are."

C. "Why?"

"Because my mom picked these out." "Mrs. Richards!" Charles whispered to himself as he scooped up the pile of clothes and slowly headed for the boys changing room. This was the first time he really looked at the inside of the changing room. There wasn't a whole lot to see. Eight feet high, four foot by four foot, a plain door and open to the ceiling above. He slipped on a pair of pants and a shirt. When he went to step out of the room he heard someone say "Alice what are you doing in the men's section?" Charles peeked around the wall. He saw a fifteen to sixteen year old boy holding a broom. 'Who is he?' Charles thought. Alice answered the boy "Oh, so you haven't met my project, Charles?" "No, your project?" the boy said. "Yes, I plan on turning Charles into a nice respectable young man, I do." Alice told the boy. Charles bit his lip he could hide no longer. He slowly emerged. "And here he is." Alice gesturing with her hand to Charles. "Charles, come and meet Dan, the errand boy for the store." Charles eyed the boy.

Dan was an inch or two taller than Charles. He had curly blond hair and blue eyes. Charles figured he had better talk fast or Alice would talk for him. "Hello Dan, Dan is short for dinosaur I suppose?" Dan laughed; "Dan is short for Daniel." he said to Charles and turned to Alice. "You didn't mention that he was a wit." "I didn't know." Alice said dryly "Dan!" A man's voice boomed from some where in the store. "Got to go. That's my boss." Dan said. He turned and ran off dropping the broom he had been sweeping with.

"Dan for dinosaur, and he laughed! Boys have no sense of humor." Alice scoffed. *This day might not be so bad after all, in fact, life in this town might not be so bad.* Charles thought to himself. Alice turned to look at him. "Go change into your own clothes and let's go find Mother, Charles" she said. Charles hurried to the dressing room changed and sped back to Alice. "Come on, Miss." he said to Alice who was still shaking her head and mumbling under her breath.

They found Mrs. Richards at the shoe section, picking out boots. "There you two are, Charley try these on for me," she said handing him some boots. Sitting on the floor Charles pulled off his old boots and slipped on the new. "They fit well." Charles said in reply when

Mrs. Richards asked how they fit. The trio made their way to the front of the store where Mrs. Richards found a friend and began to talk. Alice motioned for Charles to come on and Charles followed her a few feet away. "Mother will talk all day to Mrs. Jones, because they are both big talkers. But if Mother looks up and sees us checking out she'll wrap up the conversation and come on over." "But, but." Charles protested, while reluctantly following Alice over to the counter where a smiling dark haired woman began checking them out.

Sure enough, Mrs. Richards saw them and came over. "What are you two doing?" She asked. "Oh, just checking out mother." Alice said. "We met Dan the dinosaur." Charles said making small talk. Alice rolled her eyes. "Daniel, Alice's cousin?" Mrs. Richards said smiling slightly. "Well I didn't know he was kin, but yes, the errand boy for the store." Charles said. By now, they were heading for the buggy.

"Where's the next stop?" Charles asked. "Just a little ways down the road, we need a few groceries" Mrs. Richards replied. Charles untied the horses and climbed aboard. Charles drove, and Mrs. Richards and Alice sat beside him. Soon they were at the next store.

Climbing down Charles tied the horses to the rail out front, while Alice and Mrs. Richards climbed down. They headed for the store, but before they could even get inside, someone called out to them. "Lilly, Lilly wait up!" Mrs. Richards turned, Charles and Alice turned. "Molly, where are the children?" Mrs. Richards said, greeting her sister-in-law. "Oh, you know, Dan and Tom are at work, and Sue is with the little ones." She said catching up with them. "We saw Dan at the store." Alice informed the lady. "Which side of the family is she from?" Charles whispered to Alice. "That's Aunt Molly, dad's sister" Alice whispered back.

The group headed for the store. When they got inside the store Mrs. Richards turned to Alice and Charles and said. "Can you two shop while Aunt Molly and I talk? We'll wait right here for you." Charles and Alice exchanged glances. "Yes, I believe we can." Alice replied. Charles just nodded. "OK, then." Mrs. Richards handed them the list. Alice seized it. "We will be right back, Mother." Turning she darted off into the store.

Mrs. Richards and Aunt Molly resumed talking, while Charles hurried to catch up with Alice. She was holding up the list. "It says to get fruit and vegetables. So I guess just a variety." Alice thought aloud. Charles reached for a banana. "No." Alice said quickly. "Why?" Charles asked. "Because, I don't like bananas." Alice replied. Charles sighed and reached for some celery. "Oh, no!" Alice said. "What now?" Charles asked. "I really don't like celery." Alice answered. Charles rolled his eyes and reached for some carrots. "No." Alice said again. "You don't like carrots?" Charles asked with disgust. "Nope." Alice said.

"What do you eat?" Charles questioned.

A. "In what food category?"

C. "Fruits and vegetables, of course."

A. "Grapes."

C. "And…"

A. "Apples."

C. "And…"

A. "Oranges."

C. "And…"

A. "I'm sure there's something else, but let's start with that."

C. "OK."

Charles went to one side of the fruit rack and Alice went to the other. "Oh, and strawberries, I do like strawberries!" Alice called to Charles "Ma'am?" a worker asked. "Uh-mmm, see I was talking to Charles." Alice replied. Charles peeped through the racks at Alice, Her face was red and she was dancing about like she had ants in her pants. Charles put his hand over his mouth to keep from laughing. "Charles? I don't see anyone else little girl." The lady said. "He's on the other side of the fruit rack." Alice squeaked as she ran to Charles' side of the rack. She squatted and pulled her bonnet over her head.

16

Charles patted the top of her head and said "It's OK, Alice. It happens to the best of us." As he bit his lip to keep from laughing. Charles peeked back through the rack and saw that the lady was no longer there. "She's gone now," he said. Alice peeked out, she stood up, and they continued shopping.

It wasn't long before they were checking out. Charles unloaded the basket. The girl behind the counter tallied and Alice studied the goings on. "Hey!" Alice exclaimed as the girl picked up a bunch of bananas. "How did these get in here?" "I put them in." Charles replied "Didn't you here me say I don't like bananas?" she asked. "Yes." he answered. "Then why did you get them?" she asked sounding a bit irritated. "Because we're just not shopping for you." Charles replied as if he had already given this some thought. Alice looked surprised then she looked around. The girl behind the counter was watching her. The customers in the front of the store were watching her, most of who knew her. Then she smiled slowly. "OK," she agreed, "We'll keep them." The sales clerk smiled brightly and kept totaling. Charles smiled and kept unloading stuff. Groups of people whispered. Alice smiled and kept on watching.

Charles and Alice found Mrs. Richards and Aunt Molly still chatting outside. "Mother we're done shopping!" Alice said. "Oh, Molly I hate to run but, the children want to stop at some other stores and I'm sure you have other stops too. Goodbye" Mrs. Richards said backing away. "Oh, yes but, Lilly!" Aunt Molly called but Mrs. Richards was already climbing into the buggy. "...Talked my ear off the whole time" Mrs. Richards was saying when Charles climbed into the buggy holding the rein. "Where are we going next, Mrs. Richards?" Charles asked. Mrs. Richards sighed "Alice?" she asked. "The hardware store of course." Alice said. "Why there?" Charles asked "Dad reminded us three times this morning to be sure we get that pound of nails." Alice said. "Oh yeah!" Charles and Mrs. Richards said in unison.

It took only two or three minutes to get there. To Charles it seemed like an hour, because Mrs. Richards was catching Alice up with all that Aunt Molly had to say. Charles was getting tired of all the girl talk. When they got there, Charles jumped down and tied up the horses. He then hurried to catch up with Alice and Mrs. Richards, who were heading for the store. It took no time at all to get the nails and get out. Alice and Mrs. Richards loaded up while Charles untied the horses. Charles climbed in and they took off. Alice and Mrs. Richards were engaged in a conversation that Charles cared nothing for, so he busied himself thinking about what the rig would be like. By the time they reached home, Alice was caught up on the happenings and Charles had a mental image of what he thought the rig would look like.

When they got home, Charles stopped the horses in front of the house. Alice and Mrs. Richards hopped down, swiped the stuff out of the back of the wagon and headed for the house. Charles drove the horses around the barn and unhitched them. He rubbed the horses down and put them in the corral.

Then he went to see Chess who had his own little pen. It was a stall that opened to a pen in the back so that Chess could graze, stretch his legs and get some sunshine. "Chess!" Charles called. The horse whinnied and swung his head over the stall door. "Hi, boy." Charles said as he patted the horse's nose. Charles put his hands into his pockets and shuffled to the door.

I wonder who I should thank for all of this? He opened the barn door and shut it behind himself. Pausing he looked up at the clear blue sky. *GOD? Could it be?* Charles thought about what Mr. Richards had read the night before. It had been something about GOD creating the heavens and the earth. Was it true? Charles slowly walked toward the house thinking as he went. He had had everything but a Godly upbringing. He did not remember his dad being very Godly. The children's home was a "Christian Home" but those people were not like Mr. and Mrs. Richards. Charles was truly confused. He put his hand on the doorknob, hesitated then opened the door.

THE STRANGEST ROBBERY

Charles was surprised to find Mr. Richards in the living room. "Mr. Richards I didn't know you were home." He said. "I live here, don't I?" Mr. Richards said laughing. "Well, yes sir, but most men don't come home to eat do they?" Charles said. "No, most men don't, but the boss comes home." Mr. Richards said. "I see." Charles said because he could think of nothing else to say. "Well just don't stand there, sit down and tell me what y'all did in town." Charles sat down and told Mr. Richards about their day. "Come and get it!" Mrs. Richards called. Charles and Mr. Richards went to eat their lunch.

Chapter 3

The Rig

Charles waved to Alice and Mrs. Richards as he and Mr. Richards pulled out. Charles turned and faced the front, his stomach was in knots. What if he couldn't be enough help to Mr. Richards? Not only did he have to work enough to pay for all of his food, clothes, and housing he had to do more. He had to be so much help that people would be standing around with nothing to do. The jolt of the wagon stopping brought him out of his daze. Charles looked around himself. Four log cabins stood, two on each side of the road. One said 'office' and one had a corral built behind it and horses in the corral. Charles got no farther for just then Mr. Richards pushed the reins into Charles' hands and hopped down without a word. Charles didn't need to be told what to do. He headed for the barn.

Charles pulled the wagon up beside the barn, unhitched the horses and led them into the barn. Charles' eyes adjusted to the light and he noticed a boy coming toward him. The boy was shorter than Charles but not by much. He had light brown hair and green eyes. "Hi." the boy greeted with a friendly smile. Charles smiled back. "Hi, my name is Charles. What's yours?" Charles asked. "My name is Thomas, but people call me Tom, for short." the boy said. "Oh!" Tom said after a pause. "You must be the boss's son. He told us all this morning he was bringing his son after lunch." "Mr. Richards called me his son?" Charles asked with wide eyes. "Well, yes he called somebody his son." Tom said. "I'm flattered." Charles said. "Then, then you're not his son?" Tom said "Sounds to me like I am." Charles said. Tom smiled and the boys spoke of it no more.

"The boss said we are to treat you as a honored guest of the manager of this oil company. Then he said I was to teach you the ropes of the stables." Tom informed Charles. "Well I hate to contradict the boss, but I rather you treat me as an equal." Charles said. Since Charles was a fast learner, it didn't take him long to learn the 'ropes'. The boys laughed and talked. When somebody pulled up, they took care of their horses.

"Hey, have you ever wrestled before, Charles?" Tom asked after awhile. "Yes." Charles said bluntly. "For fun?" Tom asked. "No." Charles replied. "Would you like to?" Tom asked. "Sure!" Charles said. "OK, then let's trade punches. You may be three inches taller, but I'm the best wrestler in this part of the country." Tom boasted. "Really? Well that might just have to change." Charles said. The boys stared each other down, and then rushed toward their opponent. They met in the middle of the barn, locked up and fell to the ground in a tangle. They rolled over one another, kicking up a dust storm. Both boys bent on beating the other. The fight didn't last long, as such fights never do. The boys were close in weight, but it didn't take long for Charles to get Tom in a headlock. Tom tapped out while choking, signaling that the match was over. Charles hopped to his feet and waited for Tom to rise. Tom got to his feet and held out his hand, the boys shook hands.

They jumped when they heard clapping. They both turned to see the barn door crowded with men, Mr. Richards stood in front, clapping. Both boys blushed as they listened to the men talk. "I told you the bigger one would win." One roughneck said. "Tom's the best fighter around." Another man said. "You owe me ten cents." One man said to another. "Thomas, how could you let that boy beat you?" one man asked. "Aww, Dad he's a foot taller than me." Tom replied. The men all laughed, but Mr. Richards broke the party up with a, "Alright men, back to work." The men went back their business; the boys went back to their business too. Charles did not hold his win over Tom's head. Everyone had seen Charles win, what sense was there in gloating?

The rest of the afternoon passed quietly, with nothing out of the ordinary happening. When the clock struck six all the men came for their horses. Soon all that was left was Mr. Richards rig and Thomas's horse. The boys locked the barn and Tom headed for his home. "Goodbye Charles, see ya tomorrow." "Goodbye Tom." Charles and Mr. Richards left last. Mr. Richards was looking all around and acting very strangely. "What's the matter Mr. Richards?" Charles asked. "Oh, somebody has been siphoning oil right out of the barrels. I'm just giving the place a look over." Mr. Richards answered. "Do you have a guess who it is?" Charles asked. "Nope, but it's nothing for you to worry about." Mr. Richards said, but Charles was worried anyway.

While the horses trotted, a small breeze came up. *It was a fine ending to a fine day.* Charles thought. "I'm hungry, aren't you?" Mr. Richards asked. "I'm starved, I wonder what the ladies cooked?" Charles replied. "Not soup, I hope." Mr. Richards said. "I'd appreciate anything they'd cook." Charles said. "Yes, I guess I do need to skip a few meals, that way I'd appreciate whatever Alice cooks." Mr. Richards said. "Oh, I didn't mean that Mr. Richards." Charles said embarrassed. "I know, but I do." Mr. Richards said. Charles slumped down in his seat "I hope Mother cooks tonight. I know it's selfish of me but I'm really hungry." Mr. Richards said. Charles smiled.

As they pulled into the barn twilight was just setting in. A whippoorwill called out somewhere in the darkness. Charles fixed up one horse and Mr. Richards got the other. As they reached the house the smell of fried meat and fresh baked bread welcomed them. They entered at the door stepping into Mrs. Richard's cozy kitchen.

Dinner was a good one, with hamburger steaks, mashed potatoes, broccoli, and dinner rolls. After they had finished dinner Mrs. Richards said "Alice, clear the table off and bring on the dessert." Alice got up and started stacking plates. Charles hopped up and started helping her. After they cleared the table Alice hurried to the far end of the kitchen. She grabbed a step-stool and pushed it to the counter. She stepped up on the stool and then climbed onto the counter. She knelt on the counter and reached into the farthest corner of the top cabinet. She removed a tray covered in a tea towel from the cabinet. Alice climbed down from the counter and turned toward Charles.

Scowling, she said to Charles, "Go get in your spot." "How come?" Charles asked. "Because if you don't I'm putting this back and you won't get any." Alice said. "What is it?" Charles asked. "You'll see," Alice said. So Charles turned and went to the dining room. He sat down and stared at the kitchen doorway. Alice soon appeared walking backward into the dining room. She was looking over her shoulder, but didn't notice that one of the floorboards was slightly raised above the others. Alice's foot caught the raised board and in an instant Alice was upside down on the floor. But Charles managed to save the tray. Alice hopped up real quick. She gave Charles a look like he had made her trip, and swiping the tray she placed it on the table. Alice grabbed the napkin off the tray, exclaiming "Ta Da!" as she did so.

For a moment all was quiet, as everyone looked the dessert over. *What are they? I wonder*, thought Charles to himself, while looking at the black, round things on the tray. *They could be cookies under the right conditions. I hope Alice tells us what they are.* Charles thought

24

THE STRANGEST ROBBERY

to himself. "Well?" Alice asked. Mr. Richards looked ready to say something but Alice spoke first. "I'd prefer if Charley would analyze them first." "Um-mm, well they look good I suppose." Charles said. Alice turned to Charles and said, "Try a ginger snap and tell me how they taste Charley." *Boy, I'm glad she said what they are.* Charles thought as he bit into one. Crunch! *Whoa! I wonder if there supposed to be this crunchy.* "Well, well?" Alice asked excitedly. "It's good I think, I mean, if you like really crunchy things that is." Charles answered. Alice raised one eyebrow. "I don't understand, did you or did you not like them?" "There the best ginger snaps I've ever had." Charles answered. *I'll not mention that I've never had ginger snaps before.* Charles thought. Alice smiled, obviously pleased.

"Do you want my opinion Alice?" Mr. Richards asked. Alice turned. "Yes, I would." she answered. "Well," Mr. Richards began "First off they're burnt. Honestly Alice, I think you could burn water. And secondly, they're too big and flat." Mr. Richards finished. "I think they're very good dear," Mrs. Richards said. Alice smiled, and then hopping up she grasped the platter. "Let's not eat them all." She said. Charles gathered the glasses and followed her to the kitchen.

Alice washed and rinsed the dishes, while Charles dried and put them away. They finished the kitchen in record time and went to the living room to read the Bible.

Charles listened intently as Mr. Richards read about Adam and Eve. *How could a loving God throw these people out of the garden?* Then he had another thought, *why didn't Eve guess something was up when a snake talked to her? Snakes don't talk.*

Charles wanted to ask Mr. Richards these and a hundred other such questions, but for some reason he could not. He felt uneasy, would Alice laugh? She must know so much more than me about the Bible. He thought.

The evening passed quickly as Alice and Mr. and Mrs. Richards learned about each other's day. Charles' questions plagued him He wanted so badly to find out the answers!

25

Chapter 4

Salvation

As Charles tromped off to his room, his questions replayed in his mind. Why hadn't he asked? Charles shut the door behind himself and paced around, his mind reeling. Charles stopped before the window and opened it. As the cool night air blew in, Charles sat on his bed holding his spinning head. He suddenly jumped as a thought came to him, what if Alice could answer his questions.

Charles shook his head. *No, no Alice would just laugh.* One person in his head said. What if she did? Another person in his head retorted. What was it to him? Let her laugh.

Charles' hand rested on the doorknob. Slowly Charles turned the knob, the door creaked open. Charles crept down the dark hallway to Alice's room and softly knocked on her door.

Alice opened the door and looked quite surprised to see Charles standing there. "Why didn't Eve run at the first sight of a talking snake?" Charles asked with his excitement over running him. Alice put her finger to her mouth and said "Shh!" then motioned for him to step inside.

"What are you talking about?" Alice asked after shutting the door. "The Bible Alice, why didn't she run?" Charles asked. "I don't know, maybe a snake had talked to her before." Alice answered. "Alice, snakes don't talk. I mean when is the last time a snake talked to you?" Charles asked.

"Well, never but things weren't the same back in those days. People and animals were bigger and smarter in those days you know." Alice said. "Hum-mm, I'm not satisfied with that answer, but we'll come back to that later. Why did God throw them out of the garden?" Charles asked. "They sinned, remember?" Alice answered. "Yes but when I sin God doesn't throw me off the face of the earth, does he?" Charles replied.

A. "No but he will someday."

C. "What!?!"

A. "Ever heard of hell?"

C. "Not really."

"Well then I'll tell you about it. It's a place of everlasting torment and pain. It's like being in a fire for ever and ever, not the kind of place you'd go and hang out at."

Charles' eyes looked wide with horror. "Why haven't I ever heard of this before?" Charles asked after a moment. Alice shrugged. "Well, are you going there?" Charles asked. "Nope." Alice answered nonchalantly. "Oh, you're that good?" Charles asked sincerely.

"Me good? No, no it isn't that." Alice replied. "Then what is it? I mean, is there hope?" Charles asked. "For who?" Alice asked. "For me or, or anybody else?" Charles said. "Well would you consider yourself to be a good person?" Alice asked. "No, I mean not to God. He gets mad if you eat the wrong kind of fruit." Charles said.

Alice gave a little laugh and then said; "And do you believe there is this place called hell?" "Yes." Charles said. "And do you believe that Christ died on the cross for your sins and He rose on the third day?" Alice asked, "Yes." Charles replied.

"Then yes, there is hope." Alice said answering his question. "What do I do then?" Charles asked leaning forward. "Repent. Go to your room and pray to GOD, repenting for every sin you've ever committed." Alice instructed.

Charles turned slowly. He went to his room and fell to his knees before the window. The window was still open and a soft breeze blew in, drying the tears on his face. "Oh God up in heaven..." Charles began.

So that night Charles Wilson joined the Christian camp, and became a brother in Christ. Charles went to breakfast the next morning, his face radiating with joy.

"My, you look happy this morning. Did you have a good nights sleep?" Mrs. Richards greeted him as he came bounding down the hall for breakfast. "Yes ma'am, I had a fair nights sleep but that's not why I'm so happy." Charles said grinning ear to ear.

"Oh, why then?" Mrs. Richards questioned. "Because I did what you did, and Mr. Richards did and Alice too." Charles beamed. "And what is that?" Mrs. Richards asked. "I got saved and I'm so happy." Charles said. "Really?" Mrs. Richards asked. "Oh, yes." Charles said. "Oh, then I'm so happy too Charles!" Mrs. Richards said, hugging him.

Soon the whole family knew with Mr. Richards commenting "That's great." Alice just smiled and nodded knowingly. The morning passed quickly and soon Charles and Mr. Richards were off to work. They were the first to arrive at work. Mr. Richards showed Charles where the key was then headed off to his office. Charles whistled a merry tune while he opened the barn.

Tom and his dad rode up next side by side on their horses. "Morning Tom, morning Sir." Charles greeted. "Morning, Charles." Tom called hopping off of his horse. "Good morning." Tom's dad said nodding to Charles and handing his reins to Tom.

Then a steady stream of horses began pouring in. The boys just worked: taking the reins, taking off the tack, and putting the horses in the corral, again, again, and again. Finally the last horse was in the corral and the door was shut. Charles turned to Tom "How do you normally handle the horses?" he asked wiping his forehead with the back of his hand. Tom motioned to the smallest corral "Just put 'em in there tack and all. Then take your own sweet time putting them big corral." Tom answered.

After a moment Tom said, "Come on let's put all this up." He grabbed up a harness and hung it up on a peg in the wall. Charles followed Tom's example and the boys made short work of the pile.

"Tom…"Charles began after the two had freshened the water trough and all the other chores around the barn had been done… did you ever get saved?" Tom looked up from the stick he had been whittling into a little bird. "Yes Charles, I have. Have you?" Tom asked. "Yes, just last night I was." Charles replied happily. "That's good, my last helper wasn't." Tom said. "What happened to him?" Charles asked surprised to find that Tom had had a helper before. "He got fired for stealing." Tom answered. "Stealing! Stealing what?" Charles asked. "Kerosene" Tom replied. "They sell it at the front store. Speaking of which, how come Alice didn't come with y'all this morning Charles?" Tom finished with a question.

"Alice? What would she be doing here?" Charles asked. "Alice runs the front store Tuesdays and Thursdays." Tom replied. "Oh, I didn't know that." Charles said nonchalantly. "Why don't you go see if she's there?" Tom asked. "Do I care if she's there or not?" Charles said indifferently. "Yes you do, besides you haven't seen the front store." Tom said. Charles argued back but in the end he decided to go. As he walked down the road he spotted the store. It had a banner that read, "Candy, Kerosene, Pies and Preserves!"

Charles peeked through the window. Only Alice was there, but she was quite a sight to see. To begin with she was singing, "Amazing, Grace! How sweet the sound…" and also she was, um, dusting? No,

THE STRANGEST ROBBERY

more like dancing with a feather duster. Charles put his hand over his mouth to keep from laughing. Charles stepped forward and opened the door. The bell on the front door clanged as he did so.

Alice looked up. "So you're here. How did you get here?" Charles asked. "I walked. I yelled and yelled at y'all but you rode off without me so I walked." Alice said. "Oh, sorry Alice, we didn't hear you." Charles apologized. "Oh, that's OK, it was a nice walk, all three miles." Alice said smiling. "I'd never seen the front store before," Charles said, "It's quite nice."

Not that he was glad Alice had to walk; it was not that at all. Simply that Alice need not feel sorry for herself. Charles would give her no sympathy. "Yes, it is nice. I was just doing a little dusting." Alice said, and with that, she turned and started dusting again.

"What did you come up here for anyway?" Alice asked. "Oh, just to see if you were here. Tom said you came today." Charles replied. "Well I'd best be going." He said as he turned and pushed open the door. "Bye!" Alice called. "Bye." Charles responded.

Charles turned and ran all the way back to the barn. "Anybody come while I was gone Tom?" "Nope, was Alice there?" Tom answered. "Yep." Charles said plopping down by his friend. There was a moment of silence then "What do you do all day?" Charles asked.

"Play with the horses some, whittle some, whistle some, and answer questions some." Tom answered. Charles sighed, "Who is that little bird for?" Charles asked. "My little sister." Tom answered. "Oh." Charles said.

Another pause then Charles said "I'm bored." Tom laughed, "Not enough adventure for you, huh?" "No, it's not." Charles said. Tom set the bird aside, put the knife in his pocket and hopped up and said. "Well then let's go see what the men are doing." "Can we, I mean will anybody come while we're gone?" Charles asked. "Naw, no one ever comes to the barn." Tom said. "OK, if you think we can." Charles said smiling.

So the two boys set out to spy on the men. They crept from building-

31

to-building, tree-to-tree, and rock-to-rock. "There's the rig," Tom said pointing. "And there's the towers," Tom added. "That there is the building where they hold the barrels," Tom said pointing across the way. "What's that building?" Charles asked. "That's just another warehouse where they store the oil and such." Tom said. Charles nodded. They looked around a bit more then headed back to the barn.

Once there they freshened the horses' water and threw the horses some hay. Soon it was lunchtime. As they hitched up Mr. Richards' horses, Tom asked, "Are you staying here for lunch?" "I don't know if I'm going home or not." Charles replied. "Well, you don't have a lunch, so I guess you're going home." Tom said. "I'll ask Mrs. Richards to pack me a lunch tomorrow." Charles said patting the horse's soft noses. Mr. Richards walked around the corner of the barn. "All right, let's go." he said. "Yes, sir." Charles replied and with that they got into the wagon. Tom waved goodbye as they rode away.

Mr. Richards was looking all around like he was before. Charles looked around too. "Are we going to leave Alice here?" Charles asked as they passed the store. "Yes, she sells lunch Tuesdays and Thursdays." "Oh, you don't worry about her?" Charles asked in surprise. "No, there's a shotgun under the desk." Mr. Richards said glancing over his shoulder. The wagon rattled and bumped so they rode the rest of the way in silence.

Chapter 5

A Rope is Found

M<small>RS. R</small>ICHARDS FED THEM SANDWICHES for lunch. She had made bread that morning. After lunch Charles and Mr. Richards went back to work. "Hi, Charles." Tom called from the doorway of the barn. "Hey, Tom." Charles replied heartily as he led the horses toward the barn and his friend. "Did you have a good lunch?" Tom asked. "Yep, did you?" Charles said while leading the horses inside. "Sure did." Tom said taking one horse. The boys worked quietly and soon worked themselves out of a job, again. So they sat once again bored silly.

Tom was a whittling and Charles was a sitting. "Now what?" Charles asked after a few minutes. "I don't know." Tom said. "Well, I'm bored again." Charles said hopping up. "Goodness Charles, what do you want, me to constantly to entertain you?" Tom said looking up at Charles who was pacing the floor. "Well, yes." Charles said. Tom shook his head. "Go check on the horses." he suggested. Charles sighed, "I guess so."

Turning Charles went to check on the horses. "What should I do boys?" Charles asked the horses as he leaned on the corral fence. They, not surprisingly, said nothing. Charles watched them for a moment then turned and went back inside.

"Well?" Tom asked when he returned. "Same as always." Charles said. "Now what?" he asked again. "Oh, go visit Alice." Tom said. "What should I say to her?" Charles asked. "I don't know you'll think of something." Tom said. "Is there nothing else to do?" Charles asked. "Nothing." Tom answered not even looking up. Charles turned very slowly and headed for the front store.

"Alice I'm bored out of my mind." Charles said opening the door and stepping inside. "What do you want me to do?" Alice asked looking up. Charles sighed, "Give me something to do." "Like what?" Alice asked. "Goodness Alice, how should I know?" Charles said. "OK." Alice said laughing "Hang a swing with Tom in the barn." "What a great idea! We could swing from the loft." Charles said. Alice smiled.

Charles left excitedly with out even saying goodbye. Charles ran the short distance to the barn and bounded through the door calling, "Tom, Tom, guess what Alice suggested?" Tom looked up from where he was sitting, "What?" he asked. "A swing, she suggested we hang a swing." Charles enthusiastically said. "What a good idea, let's do it." Tom said hopping up as he spoke.

Charles nodded and the boys set to work. First they would need some rope. This was no easy task. The boys searched the entire barn, finding nothing on the first floor. They climbed to the loft, at first they found nothing, but just as they were going to give up in despair, Tom called out, "Charles, come over here I've found some." Charles ran over, "Oh, jackpot! This is just what we need." Charles said happily.

THE STRANGEST ROBBERY

"Let's get this down to the ground." Tom said, and that's just what they did. But, by the time they had found the rope and got it down, it was time to saddle the horses. "Oh well, this will give us something to do tomorrow." Tom told Charles. Then he went and got a horse and led it to the front. Charles nodded as he too led a horse to the front.

It was not long before the men began to show up. They got on their horses and went various ways, calling goodbye to their fellow workers. Soon Tom was up in the saddle also. "Goodbye Tom, see you tomorrow." Charles called hopping up in the Richard's wagon and taking the reins. "Bye, Charles." Tom called reining his horse around and galloping off.

Charles slapped the reins and headed for the front store and office. He pulled up in front of the store where Alice was standing outside waiting. Charles hopped down to help her up. "Where's dad?" she asked. "At the office, we're going right now to pick him up." Charles said climbing into his side of the wagon and calling to the horses.

Mr. Richards was just locking up when they rode up in front of his office. "You two ready to go?" Mr. Richards asked climbing aboard. "Yes, sir." Charles and Alice said together and so they headed for home.

"We sold lots at the front store today." Alice told them. "Did you and Tom get that swing hung?" she asked. "No, we spent the whole time searching and didn't find any rope till it was too late to put it up." Charles told her. "What swing?" Mr. Richards asked with a puzzled look. "See Tom and I are trying to hang a swing in the barn." Charles told Mr. Richards. "That would be a good project for you two." Mr. Richards commented.

They rode the rest of the way in silence and soon arrived at the house. Alice hurried into the house while Charles and Mr. Richards put up the horses. After they put the horses away they headed for the house.

Charles patted Chess as he passed the horses' stall, amazed at how much weight he had gained already. For supper Mrs. Richards had cooked turkey, sweet potatoes, and green beans.

35

For dessert they had the rest of Alice's "ginger snaps". Charles helped Alice clear the table, and then he dried dishes while Alice washed. They went to the living room to read the Bible. As Mr. Richards read, Charles became more and more confused. After Mr. Richards finished Charles began to ask questions. "Blood doesn't talk. How could blood cry out from the ground?" "Well, God sees everything, He knew what Cain did and he punished Cain for killing his brother." Mr. Richards explained.

"Oh." Charles said.

Then after Bible they sat around and talked about what they had done that day. Alice had manned the store, she had sold a lot. Mr. Richards had done paper work, lots of paper work. Mrs. Richards had worked in the yard hoeing and watering. Charles had manned the barn. Then it was off to bed. Charles got straight into the sack, and then remembered he had not prayed. Charles leaped out of bed and knelt before the window, "Dear God…"

Chapter 6

Tom Takes a Tumble

Cock-a-doodle-do! By the time the rooster crowed that morning, Charles was up and combing his hair in front of the little wall mirror. He had already dressed and made his bed, so he just went straight to the kitchen.

Mrs. Richards was there and she looked a little frazzled. "Do you feel okay? Mrs. Richards?" Charles asked. "No, not really but I'll be OK." Mrs. Richards replied. "What hurts?" Charles asked. "Mainly my head." Mrs. Richards said. Charles felt her forehead for a fever, and she had one. "You should go back to bed, I can cook." Charles told her. After a little persuading, Mrs. Richards went back to bed.

Charles hurried down the hall and knocked on Alice's door. No response. Charles knocked again only louder this time. "Who is it?" Alice called sleepily. "Alice get up, your mom is sick and we're cooking this morning." Charles called, completely ignoring her question. "Mother is sick?" Alice asked sticking her head out. "Yep, she has a headache and a fever." Charles informed her. "Poor Mother, I'll be there in just a minute." Alice shut the door.

Charles turned and hurried back to the kitchen. Charles stopped and looked around, what could he do? 'Well, I saw Mrs. Richards fry buttered bread on the stove yesterday, I guess I can do that' Charles thought. Mrs. Richards had already lit the stove, but Charles thought he'd better check to see if there was enough wood in it to cook. He opened the door; it looked full enough so he shut it. Then Charles sliced the loaf of bread, careful to cut them straight, and buttered both side. Charles carried it to the stove and slapped it down in the pan.

Charles watched it like a hawk, making sure the toast did not burn. Alice came in dressed and ready for the day. She took out bacon and set it to frying, then cracked the eggs open and began to scramble them. When it was done, Alice made her mother a plate, and took it to her. When Mr. Richards came in, Alice, Charles and Mr. Richards ate their breakfast.

When they were done, Charles and Mr. Richards went to the barn. Charles started to hitch the horses to the wagon, but Mr. Richards stopped him. "Let's not take the wagon, but instead take separate horses," "Yes, sir." Charles answered backing the horses away. "You can take any horse you want." Mr. Richards told him. "Yes, sir." Charles answered. He called his horse and led Chess out. They saddled their horses and Charles climbed onto Chess' back and was ready to go.

"You go on Charles, I'm going to check on Mrs. Richards and then go to work. You remember where the key is, don't you?" "Yes, sir." Charles said. Charles rode up to the house were Alice was waiting with his lunch pack. Alice tossed it to him and he caught it, "Thanks Alice, goodbye!" "Goodbye!" Alice called back.

Charles reined Chess around and galloped to work. He was there first, so he got the key and opened the barn. Tom and his dad pulled up just as Charles was finishing up with putting Chess away. "You and Mr. Richards shared a horse? That seems odd." Tom said. "I'll explain in a bit." Charles told Tom because the men were riding up one after another.

They began to put the horses up and were soon finished. Charles told Tom that Mrs. Richards had fallen ill and Mr. Richards was checking on her and then coming to work. "Oh, do you think she'll be OK?" Tom asked after Charles had finished. "Yeah, it didn't look too serious to me." Charles said.

"Good, let's get started on the swing." Tom said. Mrs. Richards was soon forgotten. At last Mr. Richards showed up about an hour late. The boys were still trying to figure out how to hang the swing. They fixed up Mr. Richards horse while he told them that Mrs. Richards merely had a cold. Then Mr. Richards went to his office and Tom and Charles went back to scratching their heads.

It was lunchtime by the time they had succeeded in lassoing the top beam. They quickly secured a wooden seat to the rope. Mr. Richards and all the men came to see them try it out. They all stood in the doorway, waiting. It had been decided before hand that Tom should have the first swing.

"Ladies and gentlemen, welcome! May I direct your attention to the trapeze artist, Tom, who will now fly through the air on the new swing!" Charles said in his best ringleader voice. Tom, who was standing in the loft, jumped off. The swing went across the barn, then back, then across, then halfway back. At that point the rope frayed and broke, and Tom landed in a heap. The men began to laugh uproariously.

Charles ran over to check on Tom. "Are you okay Tom?" Charles asked bending over his friend. "Yes, but I don't think the swing is." Tom answered. Charles sighed and glanced up at the crowd of men who were still laughing. "Uh, let's just go eat lunch." Charles suggested. "Good idea Charles, good idea." Tom said getting up and brushing off.

"Well the men sure had a good enough laugh." Tom said a little later while they were eating their lunch. "Yes it was funny, I would have laughed too if I hadn't been so concerned about you being hurt." Charles remarked. At that Tom laughed and said, "I would have laughed too, but you looked so serious, I decided against it." causing both boys to laugh.

"After lunch let's find some more rope." Charles suggested. "Another good idea Charles, let's." Tom said, finishing off the last of his sandwich, hopping up and continuing, "In fact I'm done now." "Me too." Charles said gathering up his trash and getting up. So they set off to find a new rope.

They knew there was no more rope in the barn so, they had to look elsewhere. Finally Mr. Richards gave them some rope that was not so dry rotted. Once again they had to wait. It was too late to put the rope up today, they had to saddle horses. That's just what they did, saddle 'em up and leave 'em outside.

Soon the men showed up, getting on their horses and riding off. Sometimes they waved goodbye and sometimes they didn't. At last just Tom's, Charles's and Mr. Richard's horses stood alone. "Well goodbye Tom." Charles said. Tom hopped up on his horse and reined it around. "Goodbye Charles, I hope Mrs. Richards gets better soon." Tom called back. He rode away. "That makes two of us," Charles said, mainly to himself.

Chapter 7

Mr. Richards Camps Out

CHARLES WATCHED TOM FOR A moment then hopped up on Chess. Leaning over, he caught up the reins of Mr. Richard's horse. Then he rode, leading Mr. Richard's horse toward the office. Mr. Richards was waiting outside wearing a troubled look. "Charles, I'm staying here tonight." Mr. Richards told him as he came to a stop.

"What?" Charles said completely surprised. Mr. Richards sighed and shook his head. "The robbers Charles, they're stealing way too much. I have to stay here and wait for them tonight. Now go home and get me some supper. I'll need you to protect the women folk tonight."

"Um, don't you think I should stay and help you?" Charles protested. "Nope, there's no sense in neither of us getting any sleep tonight. Better get going before it gets too dark." "Yes, sir. Should I take your horse or leave it?" Charles asked "Better leave it with me, now hurry." Mr. Richards said "Yes, sir!" Charles said throwing the reins to Mr. Richards.

Quickly, Charles turned his horse around and galloped for home. Charles made good time and was soon home, sliding from his horse Charles told Alice of Mr. Richards' plans. Alice made sandwiches while Charles filled a water jug. Then Alice packed some sugar cookies that she had made that day.

Though they had hurried, it was dark by the time Charles got back to Mr. Richards. Charles came to a stop, and then hopped off his horse. "Alice said not to eat all the cookies at once." Charles told Mr. Richards "Oh, I wouldn't worry about that if I were Alice." Mr. Richards said laughing, then he turned serious "Ya know, if I threw this at a robber, it might kill him." Charles just cracked up laughing, Mr. Richards smiled then said, "You better go home now, wouldn't want to worry Alice or mother." "Yes, sir. Goodnight, sir." Charles said, he hopped on Chess and rode off into the night.

When Charles got home, he put Chess away by lantern light, and then he went into the house. Alice was waiting for him. "I've been waiting on you to eat, Charley." Alice said, "I hope your OK with soup." "Why wouldn't I be? Did you poison it or something?" Charles asked suspiciously "No, of course not!" Alice said disgustedly. So they started to eat the soup Alice had made. It wasn't so bad, but he had been very hungry. As they ate, they talked.

"Well, how was your day Alice?"

"Fine, thank you. How was yours?"

"Great, how is your mom doing?'

"Better, she just has a common cold."

"Yes, your dad told me."

They sat in silence for a couple minutes. Then Alice asked, "Are you worried about Daddy?" "Um, are you?" Charles asked. Alice sighed, "Yes, I am." she said, "Well, me too." Charles admitted "But worrying will not do us any good." He concluded. They cleaned up, and went to bed early. "Good night, Alice. Don't forget to pray for

THE STRANGEST ROBBERY

your dad." "Good night, Charles. I will and you do the same." "Oh don't worry I will." Charles said, opening the door to his room.

By the time the rooster was crowing Alice and Charles were in the kitchen making breakfast. "I'm making a bacon and egg sandwich for Daddy this morning." Alice said flipping over some bacon. "Sounds good to me. Are you going to make me one too?" Charles asked. Alice gave him a stern look, "Have you been sitting outside all night?" she asked. "No, but I'd still like one." Charles said.

Slowly, a smile spread over Alice's face, "Does that mean you think I'm a good cook?" she asked. "Well you're much better than me, that's for sure." Charles said. "OK, I'll make you one." Alice said happily.

There was silence for a bit then, "Alice I was a thinking…" Charles began, but Alice cut him off with a smart little, "Oh imagine that, you thinking." She said laughing. "Are you quite done?" Charles asked. "Yes." Alice said as wrapped her dad's sandwich in a napkin. "Good, as I was saying, I think you should stay here until your dad gets here, that way your mom is never left alone." Charles said. "I like it, that's a good idea" Alice said.

Charles turned and hurried out to saddle up his horse, while Alice finished up the sandwiches. Charles hurried to the side door and Alice threw him a bundle. "Bye, Alice see you in a bit." Charles said. "Bye!" Alice called waving.

The sun was just peeking over the horizon as Charles rode off. "You're here awful early. Work doesn't start for another hour and a half still." Mr. Richards said when Charles stopped in front of him. "Yes sir, but Alice and I figured you'd be hungry, so I brought you something to eat." Charles said climbing off his horse. He handed Mr. Richards a water bottle and a sandwich.

"A bacon and egg sandwich! Did you know that Alice makes the best bacon and egg sandwiches both sides of the Mississippi?" "No sir, I did not know that, and I'm glad she made me one too." "Speaking of Alice, where is she?"

"She's at home. We decided she would stay home, in case Mrs. Richards needed something, she'll come over when you get home." "I see. I guess you can tell nothing has happened here."

Mr. Richards hopped up, "Hey do you want these?" he asked handing Charles a bag of cookies. "Yes, sir!" Charles said taking the bag. "Well I wouldn't get my hopes up too high about those cookies." Mr. Richards said, seeing Charles' smile. Mr. Richards climbed up onto his horse and rode off, waving goodbye as he went. Charles waved also and then headed for the barn.

Chapter 8

A Swing is Hung

By the time Tom got there, Charles had done a bunch including, sweeping the barn floor, putting Chess away and freshening up the horse water. "Charles what are you doing here?" Tom asked. "I came in for work. What are you doing here?" Charles asked. "Yeah, but Mr. Richards isn't here so I didn't figure you'd be here." Tom said. "Mr. Richards is at home taking care of Mrs. Richards." Charles said. "Oh, I see. I guess we had better get to work." Tom said this because men and their horses were already arriving.

As soon as they had put the horses away they excitedly started working on their swing again. "Go get the rope Charles and I'll get the seat!" Tom called. Charles ran one way while Tom ran the other. The rope was in the loft so that's where Charles went. Charles grabbed the rope and hurried to the edge of the loft. "Throw it down to me." Tom called up to Charles. Charles tossed the rope over the edge and hurried to the ladder. "Come on down now." Tom called. "I'm coming, I'm coming." Charles called backing down the ladder. "Are you ready?" Tom asked holding the rope in his hand. "Yep, let 'er her fly." Charles said.

Tom slowly began swinging the rope back and forth like a pendulum. He swung it a few times and then threw it in the air. The rope sailed through the air just missing the main beam and then came falling to the ground. Tom looked at it and sighed. "Don't worry Tom I wouldn't expect to get it in less than fifteen tries." Charles said. So Tom threw the rope again, he missed. He threw it again, and missed. Once more he threw, and missed. Tom sighed and said, "Well, I'm no cowboy that's for sure." "Aw, cheer up Tom, that was only four tries, which is not near fifteen. Give it another try." Charles said. So Tom wound up and threw, only for the rope to come crashing down. "Don't look at me that way, throw it again. You'll get it eventually." Charles said to the distraught Tom.

So Tom threw it again, and again, and again. "Eight times! Eight times in a row Charles!" Tom exclaimed disgustedly. "Why don't we try throwing from the loft, it's much closer to the main beam." Charles suggested, so the boys hauled the rope to the loft. In the loft, Tom's throws got a lot closer, and after five more tries Tom roped the main beam. "Hooray!" Tom cried rushing to the ladder. He backed down the ladder and Charles backed down after him. Tom was still three rungs up when he jumped to the ground; Charles was four rungs up when he jumped. "Show off!" Tom said. Charles just smiled. "OK, OK, you asked for it!" Tom said. He climbed six rungs up the ladder and jumped. "Beat that." Tom challenged.

So Charles climbed to the loft and jumped, landing like a cat. One foot, two foot, right hand, left hand. Tom was quiet for a minute then said "Good for you, Charles. I've got a swing to build." Together they tied the rope to the seat one side then the other. "That was record

THE STRANGEST ROBBERY

time." Tom commented. "Yep, took us a lot longer the other time." Charles said.

There was a pause as the boys stood admiring their work. "I don't think there's even a small chance that this rope will break." Tom said. "Me either." Charles said. "Who should swing on it first, me or you?" Tom asked. "You know, I was kind of thinking that Alice would enjoy the first swing," Charles said, "After all it was her idea." "Yes, maybe…" Tom said slowly. "Only, I wouldn't want Alice to bite the dust you know." "Yah I know, but I don't think there is even a chance that the swing will break." Charles said thoughtfully

"OK sounds good to me. It was her idea." Tom agreed. They both stood and admired the swing a bit more then Tom said, "Well, go and get her. I'm dying to give it a try." Charles nodded and turned to go but stopped short. "Why don't we both stand on the swing to make sure it will hold, but not swing on it?" He suggested. "OK, let's." Tom agreed Charles climbed on first, being careful not to swing. Tom stepped up behind him. "All right looks like it will hold." Charles said climbing down. Tom hopped down too.

"I'll go ask Alice now." Charles volunteered. "Guess I'll go get a crowd gathered up." Tom said. Tom walked toward the rig and Charles walked toward the front store. It didn't take long to get to the front store. Charles pushed the front door open and listened to the bell make a clang-clang sound as the door opened.

Alice looked up from behind the desk. "Hi Charles, what are you doing?" she asked smiling brightly. "I came to see if you would like to be the first to swing on our new swing, I mean it was your idea, so Tom and I thought you might want to." Charles said. "Oh that's mighty nice. Did you sabotage it or something?" Alice asked. "No!" Charles said. "And do you still have that same dry rotted rope?" Alice asked. "No, Tom and I both think it won't break this time." Charles replied. "Oh, OK then, I'd be honored to." Alice said.

They left the store. On the walk to the barn Alice said, "You know at first I thought you two were trying to make me fall out of the swing and break my neck." Charles looked over at her and said, "I could tell." Back at the barn a crowd of men had gathered. "Make way, Make way for Alice the trapeze artist!" Charles called out. The men had been laughing and joking but when Charles called "Make way!" they hushed and split, making way.

Alice marched down the center and Charles followed her. She marched straight to the ladder and headed up to the loft, where Tom stood, holding the swing. Charles climbed up after her. Alice sat down on the swing.

"Are you ready?" Charles asked. "Yes, are you?" Alice said. "Five, four, three, two, one, go!" Tom said. On "take off" Alice swung across the barn squealing, " Wee!" all the way. Back and forth, back and forth she swung. "Do you like it?" Charles asked her. "I love it!" Alice called back. The men clapped, Charles and Tom clapped and all in all the swing project was deemed a success. "Well we better get back to work," one man shouted, so the party broke up.

The men went back to the rig, Alice went back to the store, and the boys, they didn't go anywhere. They took turns swinging. "I'm hungry." Tom complained. "It's only eleven fifteen." Charles said from the loft. Tom, who was in the swing sighed, "I know, but let's eat lunch early." he said. "I'm not hungry at all." Charles said,

Tom landed in the loft and slid off the swing. "Let's eat early anyway." Tom said. "Go right ahead, I'm not going to." Charles said, sitting down on the swing. Pushing off Charles swung across the barn. "Naw, if your not eating I won't ether." Tom said

"What should we do now?" Tom asked. "Swing?" Charles suggested. Tom went next, then Charles, then Tom again, taking turns for a good ten to fifteen minutes. Then they jumped from the loft, skipping the whole 'ladder' thing, and headed out to check on the horses.

"They're water needs changing again." Charles observed. "You better freshen it." Tom said, walking to the other side of the corral. "I'll freshen this one." "OK" Charles replied. The boys hauled water

THE STRANGEST ROBBERY

from the creek and filled both horse watering troughs with new water. "Ya know it's kinda hot out here." Tom noted. "Yes, it is." Charles agreed. "Let's go back inside." Tom suggested. "Let's." Charles said in agreement. They walked back inside the barn.

"Now what?" Tom asked. "I don't know, swing I guess." Charles said "Well, let's see if we can both swing at once." Tom said "Good idea." Charles agreed, so they both swung across the barn. They soon tired of this too. "Well let's race." Tom said. So they raced, but they were so close, there was no clear winner. So since they could not decide a winner, they decided to swing some more. "Hey, its five till twelve!" Tom said. "Yep, it sure is." Charles said in acknowledgement. Tom jumped from the loft to the barn floor while Charles kept on swinging. "Hey, the men are coming up for lunch." Tom called from the barn doorway. The swing coasted to a stop and Charles joined his friend in the barn doorway. "Let's go get our lunches." Tom said. "OK." Charles agreed, so they went to get their lunches.

"Here's my lunch." Tom said presenting his sack. "Here's mine, with the boot print on it, thanks Tom." Charles exclaimed. "Hey, I didn't do that, but only because I didn't think of it." Tom said laughing. "Well, I hope whoever has good tasting boots." Charles said. "Why don't you go to the front store and see what Alice is selling for lunch today?" Tom suggested. Charles looked out the barn door at the store. "That's a long line." He commented "Yes, but you could go in the back door, you being the son of the boss and all." Tom said "No, that would be dishonest." Charles said, quickly dismissing that idea. "Well, how squished is your food?" Tom asked. Charles opened his lunch sack. "Pretty squished." Charles said, Tom looked over Charles's shoulder. "Who stepped on it?" Tom asked. "How should I kno..." Charles stopped.

"What is it Charles?" Tom asked. *The robber!* Charles thought, *Who would be way over here in the corner of the barn, unless he was hiding in the shadows?* "Charles?" Tom said, "Are you OK?" "Oh, yes. I'm just fine." Charles said coming out of his musings. "Well what is

49

it? What were you thinking?" Tom pressed. "Oh, nothing." Charles said simply. *I have no proof of anything.* Charles thought, still he searched the ground for more boot prints. The prints he found looked like all the other boot prints, big, like a man's.

"Let's go eat." Tom said, and Charles followed him out to the big tree where they normally ate. Charles swung up into the big tree, and sat down on one of its big branches. Tom climbed up too, and sat across from Charles. The men began gathering under the tree, talking and laughing in its shade. Charles began to slowly eat his squished lunch. Tom ate his lunch too.

They both listen to the men talk. "What's up? Why ain't the boss here?" one man asked, "I heard his wife's sick." someone replied. "You know, I was thinking that Tom and Charles should have a rematch." One big man said. "Yeah, it was kinda funny." another said. Charles looked over at Tom, who was smiling.

Looking into his lunch sack Charles saw the cookies Mr. Richards had given him that mourning. They weren't smashed at all. Opening the cookie bag he held one out to Tom, "Want one?" he asked. Tom looked up, "Sure." He said. Charles gave him one, then got one for himself. There was a good view from the tree, you could see far on every side.

Chapter 9

The Big Holdup

CHARLES TURNED WHEN HE HEARD the squeak of wheels in dire need of grease. An old hay wagon had just pulled up. There was one old man driving, he looked like a farmer. The man got out, tied up the horses, and went inside the front store. The bed of the wagon was piled high with hay; the horses were thin and old. Charles saw nothing out of the ordinary, so he turned and looked toward the corral.

Suddenly there was a scream! It had come from the front store! Everybody froze, staring at the front store. Another scream shattered the air, unmistakably Alice's. Now the men were jumping up and running toward the front store. Tom and Charles jumped from the tree and ran towards the store. It was a blur of confusion. Shots rang out, coming from everywhere.

The shots seemed to be coming from the hay, coming from behind the barn, from the derrick, and everywhere else. *The back door!* Charles thought *I must get to the back door!* Charles ducked behind a barrel. *Where's Tom?* he wandered. Crawling on his hands and knees Charles reached the next barrel. He would have to run to reach the next barrel. With his heart pounding in his chest, Charles made a run for it.

As he ran, a man from the hay wagon shot at him, the bullet grazed Charles's nose. Charles ducked behind the barrel, his heart pounding. To reach the next barrel, Charles would have to run again. He jumped out again, charging for the next barrel. Charles made it to the next barrel and looked about himself. There was a standoff at the front door. Above everything else, Charles could hear Alice's high-pitched screaming. The noise was deafening.

After catching his breath for a second, Charles made a run for the next barrel. Once there, Charles again crouched for a moment. The next barrel was a much farther run. He reached in his boot, pulled out his .45 pistol (his father had given him) cocked and fired four times for cover.

Just as he was about to make a break for it, a bullet struck the side of the barrel and oil came gushing out onto Charles. For one split second Charles froze, then he made a dash for the next barrel. Just when he thought he would make it, a bullet struck him in the leg. The ground seemed to rise up and meet him as he fell. Slowly Charles began crawling toward the next barrel.

Suddenly the barrel he had been crawling toward exploded! Charles drew back sharply, and the fire burned itself out. Pain was shooting up his leg. Turning, Charles examined his leg. Just under the skin he could see the bullet. Charles ground his teeth and unsheathed his hunting knife and made a quick cut over the top of the lump then squeezed his leg. The bullet popped out. Charles fell back, everything seamed so fuzzy!

He tried to sit up, but his head was spinning. He heard a horse whinny, he heard more guns being fired. It all seemed so far away. Slowly blackness began to creep in at the edges of his vision. The world began to shrink. Suddenly, Charles heard Alice's scream. He could not give up now, not so near the finish line! It was only fifteen feet or so to the back door.

Charles rolled over. The whole world was rocking, but he crawled on just the same. Men were shouting, horses were screaming, and Charles was crawling. Finally, after what seemed like an hour, Charles made it to the corner of the shop. Slowly, Charles got to his feet. Using the building for support, Charles waited for the sudden dizziness to wear off. After regaining his composure, Charles limped to the back door.

Charles removed one knife out of a sheath on his belt, and another out of his pocket. He put the smaller knife in his mouth and the bigger one in his left hand. Charles listened to what was happening inside. Alice was no longer screaming, and Charles could hear the robber counting out cash.

Noiselessly, Charles opened the back door. The robber had carelessly left his gun on one end of the counter while he was at the other end. Quietly, Charles put the smaller knife in his pocket, and the bigger one in it's sheath. And crept toward the gun. As he moved along, he spotted Alice. She was sitting in the corner with a sheet over her head.

Charles picked up the gun and began tiptoeing toward the robber. When he was five feet away, Charles made a leap toward the robber and stuffed both gun barrels into the man's back. The robber's hands shot up. "Lay on the ground and put your hands behind your back, now!" Charles ordered. Sighing, the man laid down on the ground.

Quickly Charles tied the man's hands and feet together. Glancing over at Alice, Charles saw that she had not moved. So he went to the front door and bolted it, (just in case any other robbers would try to come in). Still holding both guns in his hands Charles went over to threaten the man, "If your not still in this same spot when I get back, I'm going to blow you to smithereens!" That done, Charles went out side, shutting the door behind himself.

Quietly, Charles limped slowly around the shop. When he was near the corner, he dropped to his hands and knees. Creeping to the corner Charles peeked around. He quickly realized, to his great surprise, that the robbers were winning!

Thinking quickly, he crawled on hands and knees to the two old horses. The frightened horses where pulling at their rope, and with one quick cut Charles cut the rope free. With a whinny and a rear the two horses bolted. The two old horses ran at a dead run, and hay swirled everywhere. Hay, dust, and gunpowder smoke filled the air. Charles's eyes followed the wagon; every last straw of hay had blown out, revealing six men hanging on for dear life.

All the men stood, watching as the wagon bounced out of sight. There was silence for a moment, and then everyone began talking at the same time.

"Where is Alice?"

"That was a close call!"

"Yes, they were winning."

"Where is Tom?"

"What happened to the man that was inside?"

"Where is Charles?"

"Here's Tom, and he's been shot!"

All the men converged on Tom. Tom was pronounced OK., even though he had been shot in the arm. It was not a fatal wound.

"Now, back to my original question, where is the one who went into the store?"

"He's still in the store." Charles said. "Charles has been shot too." The man said. "I'm OK, I'll be fine." Charles said. "That's twelve men shot, but no one dead." one man said counting the injured men on the ground. "How did you manage to cut the horses loose? You've been shot." Tom's dad asked. "I just crawled over there and cut them loose." Charles replied. "How do you know where the man that went inside is?" Tom asked sitting up. "Cause I tied him up on the floor." Charles

54

THE STRANGEST ROBBERY

said. "He didn't have a gun? Who goes in to rob a store without a gun?" One man asked.

"Oh, he had a gun, only he'd set it down. I grabbed it and shoved it into his back before he could grab it up again." Charles explained. "Where is Alice at? The boss will be mad, mad if his little girl has been shot." another man said looking worried. "Oh, I don't think she's shot. She was in the store last I saw." Charles said. "Hey, this door is locked." one man said as he tried to open the front door of the store. "I didn't want any more robbers to come in the front door, so I locked it, the back door is not locked." Charles told them.

"I'll go find Mr. Richards." one man offered. "What are we going to do with our prisoner?" Another man asked. "Nothing right now I guess Mr. Richards will handle that." Tom's dad said. "We'd better go check on Alice. Did you say you'd left the back door open, son?" a man asked Charles. "Yes, sir." Charles answered. "Then let's go." another man said. Most of them walked around back, talking excitedly about the adventure they'd just had. Tom helped Charles along. The group rounded the corner and headed for the back door.

Charles reached out and turned the doorknob, opening the door. All the men hushed and peeked inside as Charles stepped in. There was Alice completely calm sitting at the desk. Everyone stared at her and she stared back at everyone. "You guys just missed it, someone came in here and tried to rob the store!" She said. "Where is he now?" Charles asked. Alice pointed at the blanket in the corner. "Over there. Best I can figure I screamed so loud he went crazy and tied himself up, so I threw that blanket over him." Alice told him. Everyone looked at her a minute and then started to laugh. They laughed and laughed and laughed.

Alice sat at the desk looking at them in disbelief. "Charles why are y'all taking this so lightly?" Alice asked. "What's going on in here?" Mr. Richards asked busting in. "Oh, Daddy! You just missed it. A man just tried to rob the store." Alice told him. "Where's he at now?" Mr. Richards asked gruffly. "Right over there." Charles

55

answered pointing at the blanket in the corner. Mr. Richards walked over and pulled the blanket off. He was quiet for a moment then said, "Alright, tell you what we're going to do. I'll take two men and the robber with me to the sheriff. All the wounded can go home and the rest of you, back to work."

"Who's going with you?" one man asked. Mr. Richards picked out two people and the rest dispersed back to their jobs. Mr. Richards and the two men he had chosen took the robber and rode off. Charles went home just like all the other wounded although he didn't think he needed to. When he got home he spent an hour telling Mrs. Richards what happened. She dressed his wound and went back to bed because she was still feeling bad. Charles was restless because he had nothing to do.

Come supper cooking time, Mrs. Richards was still asleep and Charles was glad to fill in for her. Unsure of what to cook, Charles went to the cellar to search for options. Salted and some smoked meat were in barrels, peppers, onions, and dried herbs hung from the ceiling. The shelves were filled with jars, canned fruits, jellies, jams and even some pickles. Charles held the lantern higher; *It almost looks like a store down here!* he thought to himself.

Charles thought of all the meals he had cooked himself. The Richards would find none of those appetizing, but they had been fine for a half starved boy: fried ants, roasted rabbit, venison, and chili consisting of some kind of meat, chili peppers and some water. Chili and corn bread! Why, civilized folks ate that, and Charles could make it. Charles hacked off a chunk of smoked meat and carried it to the kitchen. He used a kitchen knife and chopped it into small bits. Then he dropped them into a pot and began to brown them.

Charles boiled beans on the back of the stove, while he chopped onions and chili peppers. Once the meat was browned, Charles poured the beans, boiling water and all into the meat pot. Then he scraped the onions and peppers into the pot, and gave it all a good stir. "Now for the cornbread." Charles mumbled to himself, flipping through Mrs. Richard's recipe box. Once he had found the desired card Charles rounded up the required ingredients and put them on the counter. He put a little of this and a pinch of that in to the bowl, mixed until smooth, poured it into a pan and slid it into the oven.

After sliding the cornbread into the oven, Charles turned his attention back to the chili. One quick stir told him that it was scorched! After that Charles watched the chili like a hawk. While the food cooked, Charles set the table. Soon the corn bread was done and Charles set it on the table to cool.

Charles stood over the stove stirring the chili, and waiting for Alice and Mr. Richards to get home. As he stirred he thought about the robbery, he was in another world when the door burst open. "My, it smells good in here." Mr. Richards remarked. "I didn't know you could cook." Alice said looking in the pot. "Oh, I can't, but anybody can throw some meat, beans and peppers in a pot." Charles said. Alice looked at the table, "All you forgot was the molasses." Alice said while lighting a kerosene lamp and heading for the cellar.

Mrs. Richards came down for supper. After supper they read the Bible and went to bed. As Charles sat on the edge of his bed he thought about the robbery. The robber had to some how siphon the oil out of the barrels because the barrels were still there, only empty. Charles climbed into bed, *I'll think about it some more in the morning.* He decided.

When Charles woke the next morning, the sun was starting to rise and the rooster had already crowed. Charles climbed out of bed. His leg was so stiff! Charles combed his hair, made his bed and got dressed. When he limped to the kitchen, Mrs. Richards was up cooking breakfast. "Good morning Mrs. Richards, are you feeling better?" Charles asked her. "Yes, thank you, and how's your leg?" Mrs. Richards replied. "It's fine." Charles said walking across the kitchen. Charles knew he must not show weakness, or Mr. and Mrs. Richards would make him stay home. So even though it hurt, Charles didn't limp.

Mrs. Richards frowned, "Sit down, you mustn't stand on you hurt leg." "Yes, ma'am." Charles said. He sat down. Alice and Mr. Richards came to the table not five minutes later and breakfast was served. After they finished breakfast, Charles and Mr. Richards got ready for work. "Charles, just where do you think you are going?" Mrs. Richards asked him. "Just to work with Mr. Richards." Charles said hurrying out the door behind Mr. Richards.

Chapter 10

The Mystery is Solved

THEY BOTH SADDLED UP IN silence and rode off to work. Tom didn't show up for work so Charles was forced to spend the day swinging and twiddling his thumbs. For Charles the day seemed to crawl by, the hours seemed to go much slower. Finally Charles decided to go investigating. Mr. Richards had said that the robbers must have been siphoning the oil from the barrels and maybe from the holding tower also.

Charles set out to investigate the robbery scene for himself. The big door to the barn where they kept the barrels of oil creaked open and Charles limped inside. After a moment or two, his eyes adjusted to the dimness. Charles could see barrels all around. The ground was all muddy, very strange Charles thought.

The roof looked in good condition. Charles sloshed around inspecting the barrels one by one. They all seemed to be just fine. Suddenly Charles heard footsteps coming, and quickly hid behind some barrels while watching the door.

The door creaked open and a man appeared, pushing a barrel dolly with a full barrel on it; he was huffing and puffing. He eased the dolly forward to the ground, resting for a minute. Then he picked the barrel up again and started towards its spot. As the man walked toward the spot suddenly a ray of sunlight made something on the bottom of the barrel glisten. Charles looked closer it was a drop of oil, it fell to the ground and another dropped appeared.

Charles retraced the man's steps with his eyes. He looked at where the barrel had been set down and some thing caught his eye. Looking closer Charles saw it was a nail. Charles' mind was racing a mile a minute. The men were accidentally poking holes in the bottoms of the barrels with that nail! No wonder the floor was muddy! No wonder there were no fingerprints or footprints! Charles jumped from his hiding place shouting, "Woo, hoo! I've solved the mystery!"

The man jumped out of his skin and ran yelling, "Help, help! The robbers are back." Charles paid him no mind and ran straight to Mr. Richards' office. "Mr. Richards, Mr. Richards come quick!" Charles gasped bursting in the door. "What is it Charles?" Mr. Richards asked jumping up from behind his desk. "Come and see!" Charles gasped.

They hurried down to the building were all the men where gathered around. "Mr. Richards!" one man said, "They've seen the robber." "What? Where?" Mr. Richards asked. "No, no, they didn't see a robber at all." Charles said. "What?" Mr. Richards asked turning to look at him. "It was only me in there. I went in to investigate." Charles said.

The men looked at each other and then at Charles. "While I was in there I heard someone coming so I hid. I watched a man come in and set a barrel down. When he picked it up again I saw that it was dripping oil. I looked and there was a nail and that's how we're loosing all the oil." Charles hurriedly explained.

"Well, where's the nail at now?" Mr. Richards asked. "I didn't move it." Charles said, pointing to the nail in the doorway. Mr. Richards walked to the doorway and knelt down. He looked at the nail, all the

THE STRANGEST ROBBERY

men looked at the nail. It was obvious that there was a nail there now. One man produced a hammer and Mr. Richards hammered the nail out of the ramp. Mr. Richards stood up with the hammer and nail in his hand.

He shook his head and sighed, "All that oil lost, and just because the men around here are lazy." There was a pause while everyone looked at each other. Then Mr. Richards waved his hand and said, "Back to work." The men went back to the rig; Charles went back to the barn, and Mr. Richards went back to his office.

Back at the barn, Charles got on the swing. He swung back and forth and thought, "Too bad Tom missed out on all this excitement, and he sure would have enjoyed it." Charles looked at the clock and thought "I'll be glad when it is time to go home." Home? Home? Had he just thought home? *Wow, I have a home, a family, and Christ. What more could I need?* Charles thought. It was a pleasant thought. To be sure!

Watch for the next exciting adventure
of Charles Wilson in

The Strangest Escape

Coming soon!

Special thanks to my dad who typed this book up for me. And my mom who encouraged me to finish writing and not give up. For my brother, who gave me ideas when I drew a blank. For my aunt and cousin, who helped with spelling and grammar. For all my friends and family who believed I could. For all those who helped financially, by giving my brother and I jobs. Namely, Mr. Miller, the Kerzee's, Mrs. Mims, and the Parkers. And for JESUS CHRIST, may he get all the glory.

—Nicolette

To all the people on top of Gent Mt. And of course, JESUS.

—David

CPSIA information can be obtained at www.ICGtesting.com
Printed in the USA
LVOW06s1835090813

347018LV00005B/16/P